Published by Brown Watson (Leicester) Ltd.

© 1986 Rand McNally & Company
Printed and bound in the German Democratic Republic

CHRISTMAS JOYS

By Kathleen Daly
Illustrated by Mary McClain

ENGLAND

Mr. and Mrs. Mouse named their
new baby Chris Mouse, because he
was born at Christmastime, and a
happy time it was.

"Come, let's take Chris to see the
joys of Christmas," said Father Mouse.

The first thing they saw was a snowman.

"Snow falls from the sky on cold days in winter," said Mother. "Let's make snowballs!"

Soon they were throwing snowballs at each other, and making a snow-mouse with holly berries for eyes.

On the High Street, all the shop
windows were alight.

"There's a crib," said Father,
"like the one where Baby Jesus was
born on the first Christmas, long
ago."

"And there's the first mouse he
saw!" said Chris.

"Oh look!" said Father Mouse. "Our house people have made a special treat for us!"

"It's really for the birds," said Mother, "but they won't mind if we have a nibble."

"That pretty ring of holly and ivy and fir reminds people that green things grow, even in winter. It's nature's gift to us," said Father.

"My, it smells good in here!" said Chris Mouse.

"Mrs. People is baking mince pies and gingerbread biscuits for

tomorrow's feast," said Mother.
"There'll be turkey and stuffing . . . "
    "And lovely mouse-cheese for us,"
said Father, sniffing happily.

"What pretty paper and ribbons!"
said Chris Mouse.

"The Dad and Mum people are
wrapping presents," said Father
Mouse.

"And Liz and David are writing cards," said Mother. "One of the joys of Christmas is remembering all your friends."

"Now they are decorating the tree," said Father. "Right on top they put a star, to remember the one that shone over Baby Jesus's stable."

"Why are the children hanging up stockings?" asked Chris Mouse.

"If they have been good children, they will find their stockings full of goodies tomorrow," said Mother.

"Listen to that beautiful sound!" said Chris Mouse.

The Mouse family ran to their outside hole.

"They are singing Christmas carols," said Father. "Carols tell of the joys of Christmas."

Suddenly there was the sound of jingle bells.

"That must be Santa!" said Mother. "He and his elves make toys for children—and mice—all over the world."

Chris Mouse hung a mouse-sized stocking at the foot of his bed and tried to sleep.

Suddenly there was a *thump* on the roof. Then *whoosh* down the chimney came roly-poly Santa Claus.

Chris Mouse darted out of his
hole and up the chimney.

On the roof was a beautiful
sledge loaded with sacks. And in front
of it were eight tiny reindeer.

Santa came puffing up the chimney. "Ho, ho!" he said. "Off we go — lots more houses to visit before morning!"

His eyes twinkled at Chris Mouse. Then he was gone, sledge, reindeer and all.

Chris Mouse was very sleepy. He slid down the chimney and snuggled deep into bed, with all the joys of Christmas dancing in his head.

"Happy Christmas!" Liz and
David were shouting merrily as they
opened their presents.

There was a toy train for David,
with railway tracks and signals.

Liz found a wonderful robot doll
that could add numbers and play
puzzle games and talk.

Dad got a Christmas tie, all red
and green. And Mum got furry
slippers.

"And now for us," said Father Mouse.

He kissed Mother and Chris. "That's mistletoe," he said, pointing overhead. "It's good luck to kiss under the mistletoe!"

"I like it," said Mother. "Let's do it again!" And they did.

Chris Mouse stared and stared at the tiny fir branch Christmas tree.

There were ribbons and tinsels. And underneath was a lovely mouse-sledge, just right for three.

"Looks as if Santa found our little mouse house," said Father.

Just then there were happy shouts outside. Liz and David were riding their brand-new sledges down the hill

"Come on, let's go," said Father.

"And a Merry Christmas to all!" shouted Chris Mouse.